THE UNINVITED GUEST

WHEN FEAR COMES KNOCKING

LUKA T. JACOBS

Cover Design, Book Design & Formatting:
Luka T. Jacobs.

ISBN: 978-1-7637810-4-7

DEDICATION

As always, thank you to my family
for their unwavering support.

CONTENTS

CHAPTER 1

"Open it, sis," Lydia said with a smile. Kayla opened the envelope to find a gift voucher for a three-night stay at a remote property that borders the Pilliga National Forest.

"Wow," Kayla exclaimed. "I didn't expect that! Thank you so much. I finally get to go to the Pilliga, huh?"

"You sure do," Lydia responded as Kayla hugged her. Kayla's partner, Charlie, looked on, pleased, as did Lydia's husband, Jason.

"It's booked for July 20th, so only a week away," Lydia said.

"I can't wait," Kayla said excitedly. "Thank you so much. This is going to be amazing! I've been reading about the Pilliga for years."

"I thought you'd like it," Lydia said, squeezing her sister's hand. "You need a break, and I know how much this means to you."

Charlie smiled, giving Kayla a playful nudge. "Just promise you won't run off into the woods chasing Yowies without us."

Kayla laughed. "No promises! But seriously, thank you, everyone. This is just what I needed."

Jason, standing next to Lydia, added, "We all need this. It'll be good to get away and enjoy some peace and quiet."

Charlie nodded in agreement. "And who knows? Maybe we'll spot a Yowie or two."

"Or at least make some great memories," Kayla said excited.

Kayla had been fascinated with Yowies for as long as she could remember. Ever since she was a child, she had devoured every book, documentary, and podcast about these elusive Australian creatures. The Yowie, often described as a large, ape-like being akin to North America's Bigfoot, had captured her imagination. She knew the Pilliga was a hotspot for Yowie encounters and always wanted to visit and experience the area for herself.

Kayla was a web designer who had realized one of her dreams just before the pandemic hit in 2019 by opening an art supplies business. Initially, it took off very well, but after a few years of success, the business suffered and ultimately had to close. The past twelve months had been tough, filled with stress and challenges. The idea of a few days spent relaxing on a peaceful farm sounded like the perfect escape.

Kayla was looking forward to the serenity and simplicity of the countryside, hoping it would offer her a much-needed respite from her anxieties. As a free spirit, Kayla had always loved traveling and had lived overseas for a number of years. However, once the depression hit from closing her business, she had become a bit of a recluse and wanted to force herself out of her comfort zone and enjoy a few days away.

Lydia, Kayla's older sister, had always been protective of her. As the head of a non-profit animal welfare organisation, Lydia was both sensible and responsible, always looking out for her younger sibling. She had noticed that Kayla had been spending too much time cooped up at home lately and worried about her well-being. Knowing that Kayla had always wanted to visit the Pilliga, Lydia saw this trip as the perfect opportunity to get her out of the house for a few days.

It was also an ideal chance for all four of them to escape the demands of everyday life and enjoy a slower pace for a change.

CHAPTER 2

The week flew by in a blur of anticipation. Kayla spent every free moment researching the Pilliga and plotting potential routes they could take through the forest. Even though she didn't have any special equipment, she was excited about the adventure and the possibility of experiencing the mysterious allure of the Pilliga.

The day of their departure dawned bright and early. The drive from Sydney to Coonabarabran was a long seven hours, but they were all eager to hit the road. Kayla, a bundle of energy, had hardly slept the night before.

"Are we ready to go, everyone?" Kayla asked, bouncing on her toes.

"Ready as we'll ever be," Charlie said, smiling at her enthusiasm.

They piled into Jason's SUV, which was packed to the brim with supplies. As they left the city behind, the scenery gradually shifted from urban sprawl to the vast, open landscapes of rural New South Wales. They chatted animatedly about their plans, the excitement growing with each passing kilometre.

"Did you know the Pilliga is over 5,000 square kilometres?" Kayla said, turning to face Charlie sitting on her right. "It's one of the largest continuous stretches of forest in eastern Australia. Perfect Yowie territory."

"Maybe we'll get lucky and spot one," Jason said, playing along.

"Oh, I don't know about that," Kayla said, her voice wavering between determination and nervousness. "They say that when you go looking for one, you'll never see it. It's always when you least expect it. Besides, I don't think my anxiety could handle actually seeing one. Maybe from the safety of a car, with the Yowie a ways off—that would be alright."

"I agree," said Lydia. "I wouldn't want to see one up close either."

As they drove further west, the road stretched out ahead of them like a ribbon winding through western New South Wales. The sky was a brilliant blue, dotted with fluffy white clouds. Along the way, Kayla mentioned various towns where Yowie encounters had supposedly happened.

"The Blue Mountains and Wollemi National Parks are major hotspots for Yowie encounters. Lithgow has also had its fair share as well. I will put on a podcast of one such encounter after we stop for lunch."

Jason raised an eyebrow. "Some people might call you obsessed with Yowies, Kayla."

"I probably am. Yowies, Sasquatch, Dogman. It's all fascinating to me," Kayla replied. "I've always been intrigued by these stories."

"Do you actually believe they exist?" Jason queried.

"I do, even though I haven't seen one," Kayla replied. "There's just too much evidence and too many encounters from people of all walks of life for them all to be fake."

"Well, then why do you think the government hasn't acknowledged it?" Jason asked.

"Oh, there could be a few reasons," Kayla said thoughtfully. "It would panic a lot of people, and you'd have idiots going out to try and capture or kill one. If a habitat was discovered, they'd have to stop timber cutting and restrict public access. I believe the government knows about them, both here and in North America, but for those reasons and more, they don't want the truth to come out."

"Fair enough," Jason responded.

Charlie, who had been listening quietly, decided to share his own experience. "I actually saw one when I was about 20, on the outskirts of Canberra. My best mate and I were spotlighting kangaroos when we caught sight of red eyes in the bush. They were set into a large, black silhouette that was too high to belong to any known animal and too big to be a bird. The eyes blinked, and we took off as fast as we could. I've also had rocks thrown at me while fishing near there, and I've heard of a bunch of other encounters over the years from that area. I'd never go camping out there again."

Jason and Lydia both turned to look at him, wide-eyed. "Seriously?" Lydia asked.

"Seriously," Charlie nodded. "Those experiences were enough to convince me. There's definitely something out there."

They continued north-west and made a few stops along the way to stretch their legs and refuel, both themselves and the car. Around midday, they pulled into a roadhouse for lunch. The place was quaint, with a handful of locals who eyed them curiously as they entered. They ordered burgers and fries, the kind of hearty meal that seemed perfect for a road trip.

"So, what's the plan once we get there?" Charlie asked between bites.

"Well," Kayla began, her eyes lighting up, "we'll check into the property, get settled, and then head into the Pilliga the next morning. I've mapped out a few areas where sightings have been most frequent and saved a few podcasts you all should listen to. They might creep you out."

"Sounds like you've got it all figured out," Lydia said, impressed.

"I've been planning this for years," Kayla admitted. "If we are driving this far, I want to make it worth it by going to the places I have heard about."

"I think this trip is going to be good for you babe," Charlie said.

Charlie was a great support to Kayla, in good times and bad. He worked long hours as a house painter and handyman; if you needed something fixed, Charlie was your man. Having been with Kayla for over nine years, he had seen her through many ups and downs. Over the past year, he had been deeply worried about her as her depression nearly took over completely. She used to be happy-go-lucky and always up for an adventure. But lately, it was hard for him to get her to go outside with him, and he was hoping this trip would give her the boost she so desperately needed.

After lunch, they continued their journey. The landscape became more rugged and remote, the roads less travelled. As the afternoon wore on, they finally reached Coonabarabran, a small town that felt like the gateway to the wilderness beyond.

"Take a right up here," Lydia instructed Jason as they approached a turn.

Got it," Jason replied, steering the SUV onto a bumpy dirt road filled with divots and rocks. The vehicle frequently slid, struggling to gain traction on the rough terrain.

Jason, a high school music teacher, dealt with his fair share of daily stress and was eagerly anticipating a few days away from defiant teenagers. Standing at 6'2", he was a big man who rarely worried about much. Having been married to Lydia for over 15 years, they knew each other inside and out, forming a strong and supportive partnership.

They travelled in silence for a few minutes, the car jostling with each bump.

"How do people who live here handle this road every day?" Jason wondered aloud, gripping the steering wheel tightly.

"I have no idea," Lydia replied, shaking her head. "It's so rough. I can't imagine making this drive regularly."

"It feels like we're driving on ice," Kayla added.

"Okay, here it is. Turn left here, babe," Lydia said to Jason.

After five kilometres of challenging terrain, they turned onto a driveway leading to the main house. "The instructions said the main house is one kilometre that way," she said, pointing to the southeast of the property. "We need to drive past that and go through three more gates to reach our cottage."

Jason nodded and continued driving deeper into the

farm.

Kayla remarked, "Wow, this is a huge farm," noting the cows and the seemingly never-ending paddocks and bush.

"Yeah, it's massive," Charlie agreed. "I can't wait to go for a walk and explore. I might even use my metal detector. You never know, we might strike it rich!"

Kayla chuckled. "Just don't wander off too far. We don't want to lose you out here."

"What sort of animals do they have on the property, Lydia?" Kayla asked.

Lydia glanced at the information. "The Airbnb listing said we should expect to see wild emus, kangaroos, wombats, hundreds of different species of birds, and the occasional wild pig. The owner also has 600 head of cattle, but they're on the other side of the property."

"That's cool," Kayla replied, her excitement evident. "I hope we get to see some of them while we're here."

Charlie hopped out to open each of the three gates they passed through, each one creaking as it swung open. At last, they pulled into the driveway of their Airbnb. It was a charming cottage, rustic but well-maintained, with a wide screened-in veranda that wrapped around the front. The setting sun cast a golden glow over the place, making it look almost magical.

CHAPTER 3

*"*Wow, this is gorgeous," Kayla said, practically jumping out of the car before it had fully stopped.

They were greeted by the Airbnb owner, a friendly woman named Margaret. She lived in the main property on the 5,000-acre farm but was leaving that afternoon to visit her sick sister. She showed them to the small cottage where they would be staying, an old settler's cottage built back in the early 1900s. It had been beautifully restored while keeping its original charm, complete with wooden beams and antique furniture.

Margaret walked them through the essentials, pointing out the quirks of the old house and ensuring they knew how everything worked.

"One more thing," she said as they finished the tour. "If it rains, the main road into the property can get quite slushy.

I see you have an AWD, which might have some trouble, so just be cautious. Luckily, it doesn't look like rain today.

Also, there's no phone reception out here, so if you need to make a call, you'll have to drive closer to town."

"Thanks for the heads up," Jason said, appreciating the advice.

After bidding Margaret farewell and watching her drive off, they unloaded their gear and settled into the house. It was cozy, with a fireplace in the living room and comfortable bedrooms. They arranged their belongings, took a moment to admire the rustic charm of the cottage, and then gathered on the veranda to enjoy the last light of the day.

"This is really nice," Lydia said, sipping on a glass of wine.

"Definitely a great choice," Charlie agreed, wrapping an arm around Kayla.

Lydia turned to Kayla, "Margaret is really brave to live out here all by herself. She would have to be one tough woman."

Kayla nodded. "Yeah, I can't imagine being so isolated. She must be pretty resilient."

CHAPTER 4

Jason leaned back in his chair and turned to Lydia. "No phone reception out here, huh? At least there is a TV."

Lydia laughed. "I think we'll survive without one for a few days."

Kayla smiled, looking at the serene landscape. "It's kind of nice to disconnect. We can focus on the nature around us."

Jason nodded, though he still seemed a bit skeptical. "Yeah, I guess you're right. But I still need some access to technology. The TV will have to do, I guess."

Kayla smiled, feeling a deep sense of calmness. She was exactly where she wanted to be, with the people she loved, on the brink of an adventure she had dreamed of for so long. Despite her anxieties, the peace and quiet of the countryside started to work their magic on her.

After they unpacked, Kayla and Charlie decided to take a quick walk around the cottage. They noticed old bottles strewn around, a few rusted parts off a tractor, and areas where the ground had been dug up.

"Looks like wild pigs have been rooting around here," Charlie commented, examining the disturbed earth. "They can be dangerous, so keep your eyes open."

Kayla nodded, looking around cautiously. "I'll be careful."

As they continued their walk, Kayla spotted something unusual under a bush. She leaned closer and saw the remains of what looked like a small animal. "Charlie, what do you think this is?"

Charlie took a closer look. "That's the carcass of a possum. Mostly fur and a few bones left."

"What could have killed it?" Kayla asked, finding it interesting yet a little creepy.

"A wild pig, a hawk, a feral dog—could be a number of things," Charlie replied.

Kayla shuddered slightly. "Nature is really raw out here, isn't it?"

Charlie nodded as he looked at the vastness of the property. "It can be."

Suddenly, they heard a rustling noise coming from the bush ahead. Both of them froze, straining to identify the source of the sound. The rustling grew louder, and Kayla's eyes widened with curiosity.

"What do you think it is?" she whispered, her voice tinged with excitement and a hint of fear.

"Probably a kangaroo or a possum," Charlie replied nonchalantly, trying to ease any tension.

Before they could react, a small wild pig burst out of the bush, charging straight towards Charlie. He barely had time to process what was happening before he instinctively took off running. The pig, seemingly spooked, continued its frantic dash.

"Charlie, watch out!" Kayla shouted, her voice filled with alarm.

In his haste, Charlie stumbled over a root and fell face-first into the muddy ground. The pig ran past him, disappearing into the nearby underbrush. For a moment, there was stunned silence, broken only by the fading sounds of the pig's retreat.

Kayla, unable to contain herself, burst into laughter. "Oh my God, Charlie! Are you okay?"

Charlie sat up, covered in mud from head to toe, and looked at Kayla with a mix of annoyance and amusement. "Yeah, yeah, laugh it up. I'm fine."

Kayla helped Charlie to his feet, trying to stifle her laughter. "You should have seen your face," she said, chuckling.

Charlie brushed off as much mud as he could, shaking his head. "Great, now I need a shower."

They headed inside, and Charlie took off his shoes before entering the house and headed for the bathroom. Kayla gathered his dirty clothes and threw them straight into the washing machine.

The cottage felt warm and welcoming, a perfect retreat after the long journey. They settled in for the night, the excitement of the days ahead mingling with the comfort of being in such a serene place. Kayla looked around at her loved ones and felt a flicker of hope that this trip would be just what she needed to find some peace.

As evening fell, they cooked dinner and unwound from the day's events. The comforting aroma of pasta filled the air as they gathered in the cozy living room, watching TV and enjoying the warmth of each other's company. After dinner, they pulled out a few board games, eager to continue the laughter and bonding.

CHAPTER 5

"Alright, who's ready to get destroyed in Monopoly?" teased Jason, shuffling the deck of cards.

"Oh please, the last time you won was sheer luck," laughed Kayla, arranging the game pieces.

"You just can't handle my superior strategy," Jason shot back with a grin.

As the game progressed, the room filled with laughter and playful banter.

"I can't believe you just bought Park Place. Are you trying to go bankrupt?" Lydia exclaimed, shaking her head.

"Hey, go big or go home, right?" Jason replied, winking.

Kayla, chimed in, "I've got my eye on the railroads. They seem like a solid investment."

"Smart move," Lydia agreed. "Just don't underestimate the power of the utilities."

Eventually, the night wore on, and they retired to their rooms. Even though they were small, the rooms were tastefully decorated with antiques, giving them a cozy, nostalgic feel. The queen beds were comfy, promising a good night's sleep.

Kayla snuggled up to Charlie, who was already snoring softly, and was just about to drift off to sleep when a chilling sound shattered the stillness. She bolted upright, her heart pounding in her chest, heart palpitations from anxiety making it even harder to calm down. The noise was a grotesque blend of screams and screeches, sending shivers down her spine.

"Babe, do you hear that?" Kayla whispered, shaking him gently.

Charlie groggily opened his eyes. "It's just an animal, hon. Go back to sleep," he mumbled before rolling over and resuming his snoring.

Unable to shake the feeling of unease, Kayla crept out of bed and tiptoed towards the screened-in patio. The cool night air brushed against her skin as she strained to see into the darkened landscape.

The haunting sound seemed to be coming from the direction of the main house, its intensity raising the hairs on the back of her neck. Because she was not from the country,

Kayla thought that maybe it was a fox or a common animal and nothing to be concerned about. But, as always, her anxiety took over, and her mind started racing with possibilities, each more terrifying than the last.

For five long minutes, Kayla stood frozen, her eyes scanning the shadows for any sign of movement. The unsettling noise continued to echo through the night, each scream and screech blending into a horrifying symphony of fear. Then, as suddenly as it had started, the noise ceased, leaving an silence in its wake.

Kayla lingered for a moment longer, her breathing gradually calming. Convinced that the danger had passed, she made her way back to bed, her mind buzzing with unanswered questions. She pulled the covers up to her chin, the weird sounds of the night still echoing in her thoughts. Despite her lingering unease, fatigue eventually overcame her, and she drifted into a deep sleep.

CHAPTER 6

After a restful night's sleep, they woke up refreshed and eager for the day ahead. Over breakfast, Kayla broke the silence by mentioning the haunting screams she had heard the previous night.

"Did anyone else hear that screaming last night?" she asked, her brow furrowed with concern.

"Nope, I passed out as soon as I hit the pillow," Jason said, stifling a yawn.

"Same here," Lydia added. "Must have been a wild dream, Kayla."

Kayla frowned and turned to her partner, Charlie, who shook his head. "It was just a farm animal," he said, giving her a reassuring smile.

After breakfast, they got showered and dressed, excitement building as they prepared for the day's adventure.

As they finished packing their lunches and snacks, Jason turned to Kayla. "What is it you find so interesting about Yowies and Sasquatch, anyway?"

Kayla's eyes lit up with enthusiasm. "It's the mystery that intrigues me. The idea that something as large as they are exists without definitive proof is fascinating. What are they, really? Are they part human or something entirely different? It's like a puzzle that no one has solved yet."

"Fair enough," replied Jason.

They piled into the car and set off, the morning sun casting a golden glow over the landscape. As they drove through the Pilliga, they marvelled at the natural beauty surrounding them.

"This place is stunning in the daylight," Jason remarked, gazing out the window. "But I can imagine it being pretty spooky at night."

They made their way to *"The Sculptures in the Scrub,"* an outdoor gallery showcasing striking sculptures that seemed to blend seamlessly with the environment. Each piece told a story, adding a layer of mystique to the already captivating landscape.

Next, they visited the *Sand Caves*, their awe growing with each step they took. The unique formations and the soft, golden sand left them speechless.

"These caves are incredible," Kayla said, her voice filled with wonder. "I've never seen anything like it."

Charlie nodded. "It's amazing to think about how long these have been here."

As they explored, they noted that the Pilliga is the traditional Country of the Gamilaraay People. Evidence of their ancient connection to the land was abundant, with historical artifacts and sacred sites scattered throughout the park.

"It's humbling to be in a place with so much history," Lydia remarked, reading a plaque that detailed the cultural significance of the area.

Kayla nodded, feeling a sense of awe at the deep roots and enduring presence of the Gamilaraay People in the Pilliga. The morning's adventure had been a perfect blend of natural beauty and rich history, leaving them all eager to learn and explore more.

Later, they stopped at a campsite that overlooked a dam, deciding it was the perfect spot for lunch. They unpacked their sandwiches and settled down, enjoying the serene sounds of the bush. The peacefulness of the moment allowed them to relax and savour the natural beauty surrounding them.

As they ate, Kayla pulled out her phone and began reading aloud. "Listen to this," she said. "The Pilliga Princess was a real woman who used to walk up and down the highway until she was tragically hit by a truck. Now, it's said that her ghost haunts that stretch of road."

"That's creepy," Jason said, shaking his head. "I'd hate to see a ghost while driving."

Kayla continued, "Some truckers even refuse to drive through the Pilliga at night, claiming weird things happen and it's just too spooky."

Charlie raised an eyebrow. "Well, let's hope we don't encounter anything like that while we're here."

Lydia nodded. "Yeah, I don't think I would like to breakdown here at night. Can you imagine just how dark it gets out here at night? No thanks," she chuckled nervously.

The group listened intently, their imaginations running wild with the tales of mystery and wonder that surrounded them. The combination of the rich history, stunning landscapes, and haunting legends made their trip to the Pilliga a truly unforgettable experience.

As they finished eating, Charlie went for a walk around the dam. Kayla watched him, feeling a familiar ping of anxiety. Her mind conjured images of creatures lurking in the bush, watching him. She caught herself, knowing that her anxiety often tried to rob her of special moments. She had lived with it most of her life and was acutely aware of how it could twist simple situations into sources of fear.

Determined not to let it control her, Kayla decided to have a look around herself to stop the unnecessary worrying. She took a deep breath, pushing back the anxious thoughts, and focused on the beauty around her. The tranquility of the bush, the sound of birds chirping, and the gentle rustle of leaves in the breeze helped ground her in the moment.

CHAPTER 7

After their short walk, they walked back to the car, chatting about the sculptures and sand caves, their minds still filled with the rich history and haunting legends of the Pilliga. The day had been a mix of adventure and education, and now they were ready to stock up on supplies and head back to their cozy Airbnb cottage.

As they drove toward Coonabarabran, they enjoyed the scenic countryside, spotting wild emus, and kangaroos. The sight of these animals in their natural habitat was a thrill, adding another layer of excitement to their trip.

"Look over there!" Jason exclaimed, pointing out the window. "Check out all the kangaroos!"

The others turned to see a mob of kangaroos bounding gracefully across the fields, their powerful legs propelling them forward with ease.

"Wow," Lydia said, her voice filled with awe. "You don't usually see so many together."

Kayla smiled, enjoying the shared sense of wonder. Despite her earlier anxiety, moments like these reminded her why she loved exploring unfamiliar places.

As they approached Coonabarabran, the quaint charm of the town welcomed them. They parked near a grocery store and made their way inside, grabbing a cart and splitting up to gather everything they needed.

"Okay, we've got the basics: bread, milk, eggs, and some fresh veggies," Charlie said, ticking items off their list. "Anything else?"

"We should get some snacks for the evenings," Kayla suggested. "Maybe some chips and dip, and definitely some chocolate."

Lydia nodded in agreement. "And let's not forget the wine. A glass in the evening sounds perfect."

"Beer, you mean," Charlie added with a grin.

Lydia laughed. "Okay, beer too."

As they continued shopping, Lydia's phone buzzed with a new message. She glanced at the screen and frowned. "Hey, guys, I just got a text notification about upcoming storms in the area."

Jason looked up from the shelf he was browsing.

"Storms? How bad are they supposed to be?"

Lydia scanned the message. "It says we should expect heavy rain and possible thunderstorms tonight."

Charlie shrugged. "We'll be fine. The cottage seems sturdy, and we can just enjoy the storm from inside."

With their cart filled, they headed to the checkout and then back to the car, their spirits high as they anticipated a relaxing evening at the cottage. The drive back was just as picturesque, the landscape bathed in the warm glow of the setting sun. They couldn't help but notice, however, the dark clouds gathering on the horizon, hinting at the approaching storm.

As they finally reached their cottage, Jason looked up at the sky, noting the darkening clouds. "I really hope these storms don't come through tonight. Driving on that road tomorrow is going to be a nightmare if it gets muddy," he said.

Lydia got out of the car first. An overwhelming stench hit her nose, causing her to grimace. "Oh my God, what is that smell?" she asked, waving her hand in front of her face.

The others exited the car, and the foul odour assaulted their senses as well. "It smells like something died out here," Jason commented, wrinkling his nose.

Charlie scanned the area, his face contorted in disgust. "It might be a dead animal in the bush behind the cottage.

That smell is hideous."

They hurried into the cottage, eager to escape the stench just as the sun was about to set. The interior of the cottage was a welcome refuge, warm and inviting after the long day.

Lydia grabbed her camera and headed out the back door, determined to capture the beauty of the setting sun despite the smell. "I'm going to take some photos," she announced, slipping out the door before anyone could protest.

Kayla headed to the kitchen to start preparing dinner. She decided on a quiche and a fresh salad, a favourite that was both simple and satisfying. Cooking always helped calm her nerves, and she wanted to make something special for everyone.

As she chopped vegetables, the sound of Lydia's camera clicking outside provided a comforting background noise. Jason and Charlie offered to help but when Kayla told them she had it sorted, they sat down in the living room, chatting about their plans for the next day.

"I was thinking we could check out Warrumbungle National Park tomorrow," Jason suggested. "I've heard the hiking trails there are incredible."

"Sounds good to me," Charlie agreed. "A nice long hike would be great. Maybe we'll spot more wildlife. Well, that's if the roads are drivable."

"Yeah, I hope so," replied Jason.

Kayla smiled to herself, pleased that everyone was enjoying the trip. Despite the unsettling experiences of the previous night, the day had turned out well, and she hoped the evening would be just as pleasant. "After we go to Warrumbungles, I'd love to visit Hickeys Falls. It's about 30 minutes south of here and is famous for a scary Yowie encounter, she called out."

Jason raised an eyebrow. "Really? What happened there?"

Kayla walked over and leaned on the back of a recliner, her eyes bright with excitement. "A mother took her children to the waterfall one day. As soon as they arrived, they heard what sounded like a baby crying coming from the bush. They also noticed an abandoned car with its doors open and all its contents scattered around it. When they walked up to the waterfall, they heard a massive growl and were chased back to their car by the growls. As they were driving out, a police car came in to check on the abandoned car. The mother warned the officer that there was something down there, but he kept going. Later, on the highway, they saw the policeman speed past them with a terrified look on his face. She found out later that he resigned that day."

Charlie chuckled nervously. "Yikes. Those kids woud have been traumatised."

Lydia nodded. "It sounds spooky, but interesting. We

should definitely check it out."

Jason looked thoughtful. "Alright, Hickeys Falls first, then Warrumbungle. It'll be an adventure."

Kayla felt a thrill of anticipation. The idea of exploring these mysterious places with her family made her feel alive and excited. She hoped the trip to Hickeys Falls would be as intriguing as the story she had just shared, minus the spooky stuff.

Lydia returned after a while, her camera full of photos. "The sunset was gorgeous," she said, setting her camera on the table. "I got some great shots."

"Can't wait to see them," Kayla replied, sliding the quiche into the oven. "Dinner will be ready soon."

CHAPTER 8

As the quiche baked, they set the table on the screened-in patio. The outdoor setting was perfect for enjoying the last light of the day without being bothered by insects. They brought out the salad and some drinks, and soon the quiche was ready, its golden crust promising delicious flavours.

They sat down to eat, the sky painted with vibrant hues of orange and pink, which slowly faded into deeper shades as the dark clouds loomed closer. The serene atmosphere made the meal even more enjoyable.

"This is amazing," Lydia said, taking a bite of her quiche. "I could get used to this."

"Me too," Jason agreed. "Though the road into the property would annoy the heck out of me every day."

"I love it here," Lydia said. "I think I could live here full time."

Kayla swallowed a piece of quiche and shook her head. "It's beautiful here, but the isolation makes me uneasy. My anxiety would be through the roof every single day."

Charlie nodded in agreement. "Yeah. It's great for a getaway, but I think I'd miss the conveniences of town."

"And the lack of internet," Jason added.

"What I've noticed, though, is just how clean the air is," Kayla remarked, inhaling deeply.

"Yeah, when the smell of a dead animal isn't floating on the wind," Charlie laughed.

They continued to discuss the pros and cons of living in such a remote place, enjoying the food and the company. The peacefulness of the setting and the beauty of the sunset, mixed with the ominous presence of the gathering storm clouds, made for a memorable evening.

After dinner, they moved inside, content from the meal and the beautiful scenery. To wind down the day, they decided to watch a movie. Kayla poured wine for herself and Lydia and grabbed beers for the boys. They settled onto the couch and selected a light-hearted film to keep the atmosphere relaxed.

As the movie played, they laughed and commented on the scenes, enjoying each other's company. The cozy atmosphere of the cottage, combined with the warmth of the alcohol and the comfort of friends, made for a perfect ending to their day.

Kayla felt a sense of peace and contentment as she snuggled next to Charlie, her earlier anxiety a distant memory. Despite the challenges and moments, the trip was turning out to be an adventure filled with beauty and contentment.

Outside, the rain had started to pour heavily, creating a rhythmic drumming against the roof of the cottage. They were all gathered in the living room, the sound of their laughter and the occasional clink of wine glasses filling the space as the movie played on.

As the film approached a quiet, suspenseful moment, a piercing scream shattered the silence. Kayla's heart skipped a beat. "That's the same scream I heard last night," she said, her voice trembling. "It's coming from the direction of the main property."

Lydia and Charlie exchanged curious glances before standing up. "Let's check it out," Lydia suggested, her curiosity piqued despite the apprehension in her eyes.

Jason, however, remained unbothered in the living room. "You guys go ahead. I'm staying here," he said, settling deeper into his seat.

They stepped out onto the screened-in porch, Kayla trailing behind them. The heavy rain pounded against the roof, but they remained dry within the screened enclosure.

The chilling sound continued to echo through the night, competing with the noise of the storm. Lydia and Charlie strained their ears, trying to identify the source of the scream.

"Is that a fox?" Lydia asked, her voice wavering.

Charlie shook his head, his face pale in the dim porch light. "No, that's no fox. I've never heard anything like that before. It almost sounds human but it is too loud."

After a few minutes, the scream died down, leaving an silence in its wake. They stood there for a moment longer, their nerves on edge.

"Let's get inside. Whatever it was has gone," Charlie said, putting a protective arm around Kayla as they headed back in. The warmth of the living room was a welcome contrast to the cold, unsettling night outside.

CHAPTER 9

They resumed watching the movie, attempting to shake off the lingering dread. The snacks they had brought out earlier provided a comforting distraction, and soon they were laughing and joking again, the tension momentarily forgotten.

About thirty minutes later, Lydia noticed a shadow pass by the window. She sat up straighter, her eyes wide. "Did you guys see that?" she asked, pointing towards the window.

Jason, slightly annoyed at another interruption, sighed. "It's nothing. Let's just keep watching," he said. But seeing their worried faces, he got up reluctantly to peer outside. "Fine, I'll look." He peered into the darkness, seeing nothing but the glare of the interior lights reflecting off the window. Shrugging, he returned to his seat. "Nothing out there," he reassured them, though his voice lacked conviction.

Everyone tried to settle back into the movie, but the earlier tension had returned, thicker than before. The story on the screen struggled to hold their attention as they cast furtive glances towards the windows and listened intently for any more unusual sounds.

Twenty minutes later, a loud bang reverberated through the cottage, nearly shaking the walls. Everyone jumped up, their faces masks of shock and fear.

"What the fuck was that?" Jason exclaimed, his eyes darting around the room.

Kayla's anxiety surged, threatening to overwhelm her. She clenched her fists, trying to push down the rising panic. "It's just the storm," she muttered to herself, her voice barely audible over the pounding of her heart. "It's just the storm."

Charlie, ever the rational one, tried to maintain a calm demeanour. "Maybe it's just the wind," he suggested, though he didn't sound convinced.

"Something could have fallen against the house," Jason added, trying to sound practical. "With this storm, anything is possible."

"That is some pretty strong wind," Lydia said, her voice shaking. She looked at Kayla, understanding the silent terror in her sister's eyes. "But I agree with the guys. It's probably just the storm."

They stood there, frozen, waiting for another sign, another noise, but the silence that followed was deafening. The earlier laughs and light-heartedness had evaporated, replaced by a intense sense of fear and uncertainty.

Kayla took a deep breath, trying to steady herself. She couldn't let her anxiety take control, not now. They needed to stay calm and figure out what was happening. But as they stood there, the memory of the chilling scream and the shadow passing by the window lingered in her mind, a stark reminder that they were not alone in the dark, isolated countryside.

CHAPTER 10

Jason stood up, trying to shake off the unsettling feeling. "Anyone want another drink?" he asked, his voice breaking the tense silence.

Kayla nodded. "Yeah, I could use one." Lydia also agreed, grateful for something to take her mind off what could be lurking outside.

Jason poured drinks for the women and grabbed more beers for him, and Charlie then settled back into his seat. He restarted the movie, and they all tried to immerse themselves in it, hoping that whatever had hit the house was long gone.

The movie's familiar scenes and dialogues eventually drew them in, and for a while, the tension in the room eased. They laughed at the funny parts, slowly returning to the easy company they had shared earlier in the evening.

When the movie ended, they stretched and yawned, the late hour and the emotional rollercoaster of the night taking its toll.

"I'm going to make sure the back door is locked," Kayla said, standing up.

"Good idea," Jason replied. "I'll check the front."

They went about securing the house, double-checking the locks and peering out into the stormy night. The rain continued to pour, and occasional rumbles of thunder rolled in the distance.

Satisfied that everything was secure, they headed off to bed. The rain and thunder provided a soothing backdrop as they settled under the covers, hoping for a restful night.

Just as they were about to drift off, that stench hit them again. Kayla wrinkled her nose and turned to Charlie. "Do you smell that?" she whispered.

Charlie nodded, pulling her closer. "Yeah, I do. It's awful."

In the next room, Lydia commented quietly to Jason. "That smell is back."

Jason, skeptical as ever, waved it off. "Just go to sleep. It's probably nothing."

Charlie cuddled up to Kayla, trying to reassure her. "Everything's alright," he murmured. "Let's try to get some sleep."

CHAPTER 11

A few hours later, Jason woke up needing to go to the bathroom. He stumbled out of bed, still half-asleep, and made his way to the toilet. As he stood there, his eyes drifted to the window. He was barely aware of his surroundings, but something caught his attention.

Something moved.

At first, Jason thought it was his reflection. He started to focus, his sleepy mind trying to make sense of what he was seeing. Then it hit him—what he was staring at wasn't his reflection. It was a face.

He fell backward, scrambling out of the bathroom in sheer terror. He ran to the bedroom and shook Lydia awake. "Lydia! I saw something. There was a face in the window!"

Lydia sat up, her heart racing. "What do you mean?

What did you see?"

"It was dark and huge. It took up most of the window," Jason said, his voice trembling as he glanced between Lydia and the bathroom. "It had these massive amber eyes, a wide mouth with thin lips. It was right there, staring at me."

Lydia's eyes widened with fear. "What did it do?"

Jason thought for a moment, then shook his head. "It was just looking at me, watching me."

Fear gripped Lydia, but she tried to stay calm. "Okay, let's not wake Kayla and Charlie yet. Let's wait and see if anything else happens."

Jason, still in shock, whispered, "I never really believed Kayla when she talked about Yowies being real. Who would? But now, after seeing it... I still can't believe it."

Lydia squeezed his hand, trying to reassure him. "I know, but I believe you. Just take a few deep breaths and stay calm."

They sat in the darkness, the sound of the rain and the occasional rumble of thunder filling the room. Lydia held onto Jason's hand, both too scared to move, listening intently for any signs of the unknown presence outside. Eventually, exhaustion took over, and they finally fell asleep.

CHAPTER 12

The next morning, they woke up feeling groggy but relieved that nothing else had happened during the night. They joined Kayla and Charlie in the kitchen, where the smell of breakfast filled the air.

Jason, trying to shake off the previous night's tension, asked, "Kayla, do you want a coffee? Lydia, Charlie?"

Lydia and Charlie nodded appreciatively, but Kayla shook her head. "No, thanks."

Jason raised an eyebrow and chuckled. "Oh, that's right—you don't like coffee. That's insane."

Kayla laughed. "I know, I know. I don't even like the smell of it. Never have."

Over breakfast, Jason and Lydia decided not to mention the face in the window, not wanting to scare anyone else. They exchanged glances, silently agreeing to keep the previous night's events to themselves for now.

After breakfast, they all decided to spend the morning lazing around the house. The rain had slowed to a drizzle, and the occasional rumble of thunder still echoed in the distance.

"I think I'll take a walk around the farm," Jason suggested, eager to shake off the lingering unease from the night before.

"Sounds good," Charlie agreed. "I could use some fresh air too."

Kayla and Lydia decided to stay inside, enjoying the cozy warmth of the cottage. They planned to read and relax, hoping the peaceful activities would relax them.

As Jason and Charlie stepped outside, they immediately noticed footprints in the mud. The prints were large and led to the cottage, coming from the main house.

"What the? Look at these man," Jason said, pointing them out to Charlie. "They came from the direction of the main house."

Charlie paused, examining the prints more closely. "I hate to say it, but they're way too big to be human," he said, his voice tinged with nervousness. "They couldn't be from a Yowie, could they? Like, what are the odds we encounter one out here?" He chuckled nervously, looking around the farm.

Jason, trying to think rationally, shook his head. "Let's follow them and see where they lead."

As they walked, Jason decided to share what he had seen the night before. "Charlie, I need to tell you something. Last night, I saw a face in the bathroom window."

Charlie's eyes widened. "A face? What did it look like?"

Jason described the dark, huge face with massive amber eyes and a wide mouth with thin lips. "It was just watching me. Please don't say anything to Kayla. I don't want to scare her."

Charlie nodded, his expression serious. "Alright. I won't say anything."

They continued to follow the footprints, the mud squelching under their boots. The closer they got to the main house, the more uneasy they felt. As they reached the property, they were greeted with a scene of chaos. The windows of the main house were smashed, and the patio furniture was thrown all over the yard.

"Jesus," Charlie muttered. "What the hell happened here?"

Jason shook his head, taking in the destruction. "It looks like someone, or something, went on a rampage," he said, his eyes scanning the chaos around them.

They walked around the outside of the house, taking in the extent of the destruction. Charlie glanced around and said, "Margaret—is that the homeowner's name? She isn't going to be happy when she gets back tomorrow. I hope she doesn't think we did this."

Jason sighed. "Maybe there were people around last night. Maybe they're the ones who slapped the house and were watching me in the bathroom." But as he said it, he knew that wasn't what he truly saw in the window.

As they continued their inspection, Jason stopped abruptly and pointed up a tree. "Bet you've never seen that before."

Charlie looked up and saw a lawn chair stuck in the branches of a gum tree. "Holy crap," Charlie said. "I don't like the look of that."

"Neither do I," Jason replied, his voice filled with concern.

"Let's head back," Jason said quietly.

Charlie nodded in agreement. With a last glance at the chaos, they turned and made their way back to the cottage, the deep feeling of dread following them with every step. The morning light brought no comfort, only a stark reminder that something strange and dangerous was on the property with them.

CHAPTER 13

Jason and Charlie returned to the cottage, their minds still replaying what they had seen. As they approached the enclosed patio, they saw Kayla and Lydia had moved outside to lounge on the patio sofas, enjoying listening to the rain on the tin roof while immersed in their books.

"How was your walk?" Lydia asked, looking up from her book.

The guys exchanged glances before Jason spoke. "We need to tell you what we saw at the main house."

Kayla and Lydia put down their books, their expressions turning serious. "What did you see?" Kayla asked, her voice tinged with worry.

"The windows were smashed, and the patio furniture was thrown all over the yard," Charlie explained. "It looked like someone—or something—had a massive hissy fit.

Lydia's eyes widened. "What do you mean? Who would do that?"

Jason sighed. "We don't know. There was even a chair stuck up a tree."

Kayla stood up, her mind racing. "Before you continue, I'll make some coffee first," she said, heading to the kitchen. "We need to think this through."

While Kayla made coffee for everyone and a hot chocolate for herself, Jason and Charlie took off their jackets and hung them up to dry. They then took seats on the sofas, watching the rain drizzle outside, each lost in their thoughts.

"So much for the forecast of no rain," Charlie muttered, glancing out the window at the persistent drizzle.

When Kayla returned with the drinks, she handed them out, and they all settled in, looking out at the farm. "Okay, let's talk about what we should do next," Kayla said, trying to steady her breathing.

Jason took a sip of his coffee before speaking. "We also found large footprints in the mud, leading from the direction of the main house to here."

"It's either someone, or a group of people, playing a nasty prank on us, or it's an actual bloody Yowie," Charlie said, shaking his head in disbelief.

They all sat in silence for a few minutes, each pondering their predicament.

Kayla remembered something the owner had mentioned when they arrived. "The owner told us that heavy rain would make the road too hard to drive on without a four-wheel drive."

Kayla looked out the window, her brow furrowing. "Please tell me she was just exaggerating."

Jason shook his head emphatically. "Unfortunately not. We walked on the muddy road up to the main house, and it was a mess. There's no way we could drive out without ending up in a ditch or stuck in the mud. At least here we are comfortable. If we get stuck out there, we are sitting ducks, not to mention it would be damn cold."

Lydia suggested, "Maybe we could walk?"

Jason shook his head and pointed to the muddy paddocks visible through the windows. "Look at the grass and mud. There's no way we could walk through the paddocks, even with gumboots. You'd get bogged down. We had at least four inches of rainfall overnight I would say, and I'm no weatherman."

Kayla's anxiety spiked as she looked around at her friends. "Well, what the hell do we do?"

Charlie tried to stay calm. "We don't have much choice other than to stay where we are and hope it clears up soon."

Lydia frowned. "What about calling for help?"

Jason shook his head. "There's no reception on the farm, remember? We're on our own."

"Ah crap," Kayla replied, disappointed.

"Look, we only have one more night here," Charlie said, trying to reassure them. "The owner gets back tomorrow. When she does, we can ask her for help getting the car out of here. Let's just stick to what we've been doing, and we'll be fine."

They all felt the weight of the isolation pressing down on them. The idea of staying put in a place where something or someone had caused so much destruction was unsettling, but they had no other option.

The girls continued reading their books, trying to immerse themselves in their stories and forget about the dread lingering in their minds. Kayla turned the pages of her novel slowly, trying to focus on the plot but finding her thoughts drifting back to the ominous events of the morning. Lydia, usually engrossed in her thrillers, found herself rereading paragraphs, her mind unsettled by the unknown threat.

Meanwhile, the guys decided to watch football on TV, hoping the familiar rhythm of the game would provide a welcome distraction. Jason sat on the edge of the couch, his eyes fixed on the screen, focused solely on the game. Charlie tried to get into the game, but his enthusiasm felt forced, a thin veneer over the anxiety bubbling beneath.

All of them tried to put the dread out of their minds and enjoy the afternoon, but the underlying tension was unmistakable. The occasional glances out the window, the forced cheering at a particularly good play, and the brief, silent exchanges between them all betrayed their shared unease.

Kayla briefly put her book down and turned to Lydia. "Maybe we should try and drive out," she suggested.

Lydia shook her head. "It's not worth it. Think about what it would be like to be stuck out there in the dark. It would be worse than here."

Kayla sighed. "I know, I'm just feeling anxious."

Lydia reached out and squeezed Kayla's hand. "Everything is going to be okay. If it is a Yowie, it didn't try coming into the house last night, did it?"

Despite their best efforts, the shadow of fear loomed large, casting a dampener on their attempts at normalcy.

CHAPTER 14

By late afternoon, the girls had joined the men in the living room. "Let's watch a movie or play some games," Kayla offered, grateful for the distraction. They settled in, deciding to keep themselves occupied with a light-hearted movie, hoping it would lighten the mood.

As the movie played, they laughed and joked, trying to push the fear to the back of their minds. The rain continued to tap against the windows, but inside, the warmth of the heater and the comfort of each other's company brought a semblance of calmness.

About halfway through the second movie, Jason got up to make some toasted sandwiches for dinner.. He brought the sandwiches back to the living room, and they ate while continuing to watch the movie.

Charlie took a bite and smiled. "Damn, these are really

good, bro. Thanks for making them."

"Yeah, thanks," everyone else echoed, grateful for the small comfort.

"I'm surprised they taste so good," Kayla commented with a playful jab at her brother-in-law.

As Kayla ate her sandwich, she wondered aloud, "I wonder how old this cottage is."

Lydia looked up from her plate. "I read in the listing that a man built it for his family back in 1908. It's been added onto and updated ever since."

"Wow," Kayla said, impressed. "That's over a century old. It still looks fairly good though, except the floorboards. They are a little bouncy."

As they continued watching, the storm outside seemed to intensify, with the rain beating harder against the windows and occasional flashes of lightning illuminating the darkened sky. Lydia found it increasingly difficult to focus on the movie. She glanced around the room, noticing how the shadows seemed to grow and shift with each flash of lightning.

Suddenly, a loud crack echoed through the house, followed by the sound of a tree crashing to the ground outside. Lydia sat up straighter, her eyes wide. "Did you guys hear that?" she asked, looking in the direction of the window.

Kayla replied warily, "I think everyone heard that."

Charlie added, "Yeah, it sounded like a tree falling in the storm. I wouldn't worry about it."

Lydia and Kayla exchanged worried glances, the unsettling noise lingering in their minds.

Everyone tried to settle back into the movie, but the unease remained. The story on the screen struggled to hold their attention as they cast furtive glances towards the windows and listened intently for any more unusual sounds.

After the movie, they pulled out a trivia game and played for hours, their competitive spirits and laughter filling the cottage.

It was late by the time they decided to call it a night. They double-checked the locks and windows once more before heading to bed. The rain had slowed to a drizzle, and occasional rumbles of thunder still echoed in the distance.

CHAPTER 15

The house was cloaked in darkness, the only sounds being the soft snores of the sleeping occupants and the occasional creak of the old wood settling. The stillness of the night was suddenly shattered by a series of soft, scuttling noises overhead. Kayla and Charlie woke up first, hearts pounding as they listened intently.

"Babe, what is that?" Kayla whispered to Charlie, her voice trembling slightly.

In the other room, Lydia and Jason were also stirring. Lydia sat up, listening intently. "Jason, do you hear that?" she whispered.

Jason groaned and rolled over, pulling the blanket up to his chin. "It's probably just a possum. Go back to sleep."

Lydia sat up, shaking her head. "That's too big to be a

possum, Jason. Listen to it."

The sounds grew louder, the scuttling turning into heavy thumps that seemed to reverberate through the entire house. A loud thump followed, as if something heavy had jumped off the roof and landed with a resounding crash.

Lydia got up, listening intently. "Jason, you had to hear that thump," she whispered.

Jason groaned and rolled over, annoyed at being woken. "No. Just ignore it."

But Lydia couldn't ignore the sounds. She crept into Kayla's room, knowing her sister would have heard them too.

Kayla sat on the edge of the bed, trying to calm her racing heart. Charlie was already on his feet, peering out the window. Lydia put a reassuring arm around Kayla, whispering soothing words.

Charlie, glancing nervously at Kayla, asked, "Do you think it's a Yowie?"

Kayla swallowed hard, her eyes wide with fear. "Yes, I can't believe it, but everything that's happening is textbook Yowie behaviour."

Jason, now fully awake, swung his legs over the side of the bed, stood up and groggily walked into the other bedroom. "Alright, everyone stay calm. We need to figure out what's going on."

As they gathered their thoughts, Charlie, still looking out the window, muttered, "I wonder if it's the same one Jason saw last night."

Kayla's head snapped towards Charlie. "Jason saw a Yowie?" she asked, her voice trembling.

Jason shot Charlie a look but then nodded. "Yeah, I saw something last night. A face in the bathroom window. It was dark and huge, staring right at me."

Lydia nodded, already knowing the details. "We didn't want to scare you, Kayla."

Kayla's eyes widened in shock. "I think I am already scared."

"We didn't want to add to your anxiety," Lydia said softly. "But now it seems like it is back again."

They all crept to the living room, their anxiety heightened. Charlie cautiously approached the kitchen window, his eyes scanning the darkness outside. As he peered through the glass, he suddenly froze, his face draining of colour.

"What is it?" Jason asked, his voice barely above a whisper.

Charlie turned slowly, his eyes wide with fear. "It's... it's on the other side of the SUV. It's freakin' huge. That thing has to be at least nine feet tall."

The others exchanged fearful glances. "Are you sure?" Lydia asked, her voice trembling.

Charlie nodded, unable to tear his eyes away from the window. "Yes. It's just standing there. Its eyes are glowing, and it's towering over the SUV. It's just standing there swaying."

Kayla clutched her stomach, feeling a wave of nausea at the thought of the creature's immense size. "This can't be happening," she muttered, trying to steady her breath.

Jason, his mind racing, looked around the room. "Everyone stay calm. Have a look around and find something you can use as a weapon, just in case."

The group moved to the centre of the room, each grabbing whatever they could find to use as a weapon. Jason found a sturdy broomstick, Charlie clutched a heavy frying pan, and Kayla gripped a large kitchen knife, her knuckles white with fear. Lydia picked up a fireplace poker, holding it tightly.

"I'd feel a whole lot better if I were holding a 12-gauge shotgun right now," Charlie remarked.

Outside, a series of heavy thumps reverberated through the house. Something was banging on the outside, moving from the kitchen, around to the back, then the sides, and finally stopping right outside the living room.

The creature's heavy breathing was now audible—a deep, raspy sound, like someone with massive lungs suffering from a terrible cold. The group sat in terrified silence, every muscle tense, as the breathing grew louder and closer.

Kayla clung to Charlie, trying to steady her nerves. Lydia put a reassuring arm around Kayla, whispering that everything would be okay, though her own voice betrayed her fear.

The banging continued, circling the house with deliberate slowness, each thud echoing louder than the last. It stopped right outside the living room, the walls vibrating with the force of the creature's presence. The heavy, chilling breaths echoed through the house, leaving the group in a state of frozen terror, unsure of what their next move should be.

CHAPTER 16

Kayla sat in the living room, trying to think logically despite the overwhelming fear gripping her. Her anxiety refused to die down, despite her breathing exercises. She took a deep breath and spoke up, her voice steady but strained. "Okay, we need to consider our options. We can stay where we are and wait it out, try to make a run for the car, or..."

"There's no way the SUV will make it on that road," Charlie interrupted, shaking his head. "We'll get bogged, and with that thing out there..."

"And we can't call for help," Lydia added, glancing at her phone. The screen displayed "No Service," mocking their isolation. "No reception out here. We're stuck in this cottage."

Jason paced the room, frustration and fear etched into

his features. He felt a desperate need to act, to do something to protect his friends and family. "Then what do we do? We can't just sit here and do nothing."

As if on cue, they heard scratching sounds on the wall directly next to where Charlie was sitting. The noise was like nails on a chalkboard, making their skin crawl. Charlie jumped up, fear etched on his face, and moved away from the wall.

Jason looked at the group, his face set with determination. "Should I go out and confront it? Maybe try to scare it off?"

"Hell no!" Kayla almost shouted, her eyes wide with fear. The thought of Jason facing that thing alone was unbearable. "You may the biggest of us but it's obviously mad at us for some reason. We can't risk it."

Lydia nodded in agreement, gripping the fireplace poker tightly. Her knuckles were white, and her hands trembled. "Hun, we need to stay together. Going out there alone is too dangerous."

The scratching continued, growing louder and more insistent. The group huddled together, eyes darting around the room, hearts pounding in their chests. The oppressive tension in the room was like a heavy weight pressing down on them.

Suddenly, Kayla's eyes lit up with an idea. "What if we turn on the SUV alarm? It's loud, and maybe it'll scare the

Yowie away."

Charlie looked at her, considering the suggestion. It was a long shot, but they had to try something. "It's worth trying. But how do we trigger it from in here?"

Jason grabbed the keys off the table, his hand trembling. "I have the keys. I can hit the panic button from the window."

He moved cautiously to the window, his heart hammering in his chest. Taking a deep breath, he pressed the panic button on the remote. The SUV's alarm blared to life, piercing the quiet night with its loud, jarring noise. The group waited, tense and hopeful that the sudden noise would drive the creature away.

For a moment, it seemed to work. The scratching stopped, and the only sound was the blaring alarm. Relief began to wash over them, but it was short-lived. A deep, guttural growl echoed through the night, making their blood run cold. The Yowie wasn't scared; it was enraged.

Kayla's heart sank. She had hoped the alarm would work, but now they were in even more danger. "Did I just make it worse?" she whispered, fear evident in her voice.

With a sudden, violent crash, the sound of shattering glass filled the air. Everyone jumped, and Jason rushed to the kitchen window to see what had happened. His face paled as he saw the outside barbecue grill had been thrown through the windshield of the SUV.

"It threw the BBQ through my damn windscreen," Jason said, his voice a mix of anger and fear. "We need to come up with a plan, and fast."

The group exchanged fearful glances, the weight of their situation settling heavily on them.

Lydia moved closer to Kayla, trying to offer comfort. "We'll figure something out."

Kayla nodded, though she felt far from reassured. "What if it gets inside? What then?"

Charlie, still holding the car keys, stared at the shattered SUV. "We need to barricade the doors and windows. Make it as hard as possible for it to get in."

Jason nodded. "Alright, everyone grab something heavy. We'll start with the front door."

"Move, now!" Jason urged, his voice cutting through the paralysing fear. "That thing is right outside."

They quickly worked together, using furniture, tools, and anything else they could find to strengthen their barricades. Jason and Charlie pushed a bookshelf against the living room window, while Lydia and Kayla moved the dining table to block the front door.

"We need a plan," Kayla said, her voice trembling but determined. "We can't just wait here and hope it goes away."

Lydia nodded, her eyes scanning the room for anything

useful. "What do you suggest, Kayla? You know the most about Yowies."

Kayla took a deep breath, recalling everything she had learned about Yowies. "Yowies are territorial. They're known to be very protective of their area. Sometimes, certain rituals or offerings can calm them down or make them leave."

Charlie, his face pale, asked, "What kind of rituals?"

Kayla quickly gathered her thoughts. "Yowies respect certain offerings, like food or symbolic items that represent peace. We might be able to create a makeshift offering."

Jason looked around the cluttered room. "Alright, what do we need?"

"We'll need to gather some food items, preferably something natural or raw. Also, any old items that might have some spiritual significance," Kayla explained.

They rummaged through the cottage, finding a few apples, some nuts, and an old, carved wooden figurine. Kayla arranged them on a tray, hoping it would be enough.

"We should place this just outside the back door," Kayla suggested.

As they prepared to execute their plan, the creature's growls grew louder, its frustration unmistakable. The group moved with renewed urgency, their fear momentarily eclipsed by a glimmer of hope.

Jason carefully unlocked the back door and peered out. "It's clear for now. Let's go."

They moved as quietly as possible, with Kayla leading the way and placing the offering just outside the door.

The moment the offering was placed, she retreated back inside, her heart jumping out of her chest. Jason quickly shut the door, and they reinforced it with a heavy cabinet they had dragged over from the hallway. They listened intently, hoping for a sign that their plan was working.

CHAPTER 17

For a few tense minutes, nothing happened. Then, they heard the Yowie approach the offering. Its growls softened as it investigated, and they could hear it sniffing around. For a moment, they dared to hope that it might accept the peace offering.

But the hope was short-lived. A sudden, furious roar shattered the silence, followed by the sound of the offering being smashed against the house. The Yowie was more enraged than ever.

Jason clenched his fists. "Fuck's sake. Maybe there's something else we can try."

Back in the living room, they gathered again, the sense of urgency even greater now. "We need to fortify this place more," Lydia said. "Make it as impenetrable as possible."

Jason nodded. "Everyone, grab anything you can find. It will at least slow it down."

They moved quickly, using more furniture, tools, and anything else they could find to strengthen their barricades. As they worked, the Yowie's growls and heavy footsteps circled the house, a constant reminder of the danger lurking just outside.

Minutes felt like hours as they waited, the tension in the room almost suffocating. The sounds outside had ceased, but the silence was even more unnerving. It was as if the creature was toying with them, building the suspense before its next move.

Finally, the silence was broken by a low, rumbling growl that seemed to vibrate through the very walls of the cottage. The group tensed, their fear spiking once more. The growl was followed by a series of heavy footsteps, moving slowly around the perimeter of the house.

Kayla closed her eyes, trying to calm herself. She focused on her breathing, willing herself to remain steady. She couldn't afford to lose it now, not when they needed to stay strong.

Charlie watched her, feeling a swell of pride at her bravery. He reached out and took her hand, giving it a reassuring squeeze. "We're going to get through this," he said softly. "We just have to keep our heads."

The footsteps stopped suddenly, right outside the living room window. The group held their breath, the anticipation almost unbearable. The creature's heavy breathing was audible once again, it was way too close for comfort.

Kayla closed her eyes and silently prayed that they would be alright. The last thing she wanted was to see the Yowie in person; she knew she would never be able to get its face out of her mind.

The silence stretched on, each second feeling like an hour. Jason stood up from the couch and stepped closer to the wall to see if he could hear anything. Just then, the window shattered near him, glass flying inward as the creature made its move. The force of the impact knocked the bookshelf they had placed against the window to the floor, books and debris scattering everywhere. The group scrambled back, their makeshift weapons at the ready.

"Jason, are you okay?" Lydia asked, rushing to his side. She noticed a few cuts on his arms from the flying glass.

"I'm fine," Jason replied, wincing as he glanced at the small cuts. He and Charlie moved to the front, brandishing their weapons and yelling at the creature. "Fuck off!" Jason shouted, trying to sound as intimidating as possible. "Leave us alone!"

"Get the hell out of here!" Charlie echoed, his voice cracking slightly but filled with determination. "Go back to whatever hell you came from!"

The creature turned its head to look directly at Charlie, its eyes locking onto him with a malevolent intensity. Charlie's mind raced with fear and disbelief as he stared into its glowing eyes, filled with rage. So many thoughts raced through his mind: What exactly was this thing? Was it just an animal? Yet it seemed too intelligent to be merely an animal. Was it part human? Why was it harassing them?

The creature's growl filled the room, a deep, sonorous sound that seemed to shake the very foundation of the cottage. It loomed in the shattered window, its gaze fixed on Charlie, who couldn't shake the terrifying thought that they were all in grave danger.

Kayla felt like her heart was about to jump out of her chest as she stared at the creature, her mind struggling to comprehend its sheer size and power. It was a nightmare come to life, a dark legend standing before them in the flesh. She wished she hadn't looked at it.

Lydia, seeing an opportunity, grabbed a glass candle from the table and hurled it at the Yowie with all her might. The candle struck the creature right on the nose. It made a surprised "humph" noise and retreated from the window.

The group couldn't believe it. They almost chuckled nervously at Lydia's great aim.

"Holy shit!" Charlie said, a grin breaking through his fear. "Nice shot, Lydia!"

Lydia, her hands still trembling, managed a weak smile. "I just... I just wanted it to stop."

The heavy, raspy breaths of the creature filled the air outside, but it was moving away. Intense fear remained, but the immediate threat seemed to have lessened, giving them a moment of respite and a sliver of hope.

CHAPTER 18

"Jason, help me with this!" Charlie yelled, urgency and fear in his voice. He struggled to lift a more solid bookshelf, his eyes darting to the shattered window.

Jason rushed over, grabbing the other side of the bookshelf. Together, they heaved it up and moved it toward the window, their muscles straining with the effort. Glass crunched under their feet as they worked, their breaths coming in short, sharp gasps.

"We need to make sure this holds," Jason said, his voice tight with strain. "We can't let that thing come in."

They pushed the bookshelf against the window frame, using broken furniture and debris to brace it securely. Lydia and Kayla joined in, handing them anything that could help reinforce the barricade.

Once the window was covered, they stepped back, taking a moment to catch their breath. The room was a mess of overturned furniture and scattered belongings, the aftermath of their desperate attempts to fortify the cottage.

"Is everyone okay?" Lydia asked, her voice shaking. She looked around at the others, checking for any signs of injury.

"We're fine," Kayla replied, though her hands were still shaking. "But we can't keep this up forever. We need a new plan."

Jason nodded, wiping sweat from his brow. "We have to find a way to drive it away for good."

They sat on the couch together, trying to come up with a strategy. Fear and exhaustion weighed heavily on them, but they knew they couldn't give up.

Kayla, using her knowledge of Yowies, suggested, "We can't make loud noises. That only seems to make it angrier. We need to think of something else."

"What about light?" Lydia asked. "Maybe it's sensitive to light."

Jason considered this. "It's worth a try, but we don't have much in terms of powerful lights."

While searching the cottage for supplies, Charlie stumbled upon an old, hidden door behind a dusty tapestry. "Hey, guys, check this out," he called, pulling the tapestry aside.

They crowded around, their curiosity piqued. Jason pushed the door open, revealing a small, hidden room filled with old tools, lanterns, and a few boxes of supplies.

"Looks like we just found a lifeline," Jason said, a glimmer of hope in his eyes. "Let's see what we can use."

They quickly rummaged through the hidden stash, finding lanterns, candles, and an old, but functional, generator. It was a small victory, but it gave them the boost they needed to keep going.

"Okay," Jason said, his voice steadying. "Let's use what we've got to make this place as secure as possible. We can also try using the lights to keep it at bay."

As they set to work, the overwhelming fear that had gripped them began to ease, replaced by a renewed determination. They knew the Yowie was still out there, but they were no longer just sitting ducks. They were ready to fight back and protect each other, no matter what it took.

While setting up the lights, Kayla noticed a few old flares in one of the boxes. "These might come in handy," she said, holding them up.

Jason nodded. "Oh hell yeah. We can use them if it gets too close."

As they continued to work, a plan began to form. They would use the lanterns and candles to light up the inside of the cottage and the flares to keep the Yowie at a distance if it tried to approach again.

The group gathered in the living room, the lanterns casting a warm, steady glow. It was a stark contrast to the darkness outside. They could still hear the heavy breaths of the Yowie, but for now, it seemed to be keeping its distance.

Hours passed, each one stretching on. The tension was almost suffocating, but the group remained alert, ready for any sign of the Yowie's return.

Suddenly, they heard a loud crash from the back of the house. The Yowie was trying a different approach. Jason and Charlie grabbed their weapons and moved towards the noise, ready to defend their fragile sanctuary.

"Stay here," Jason instructed Lydia and Kayla. "We'll check it out."

As they cautiously approached the back of the house, they saw the Yowie attempting to break through a weak spot in the wall. The creature's sheer strength was terrifying, but they couldn't let fear paralyse them.

"Get the flares ready," Jason whispered to Charlie. "We might need them."

Just as they prepared to light the flares, the Yowie noticed their approach. With a menacing growl, it turned its attention towards them, eyes glowing with rage. Charlie quickly ignited a flare, the bright light causing the creature to recoil slightly.

"Stay back!" Charlie shouted, waving the flare towards the Yowie. "You're not getting in here asshole!"

The creature hesitated, seemingly unsure of how to proceed. It let out a frustrated roar, but the light from the flare kept it at bay. After a tense standoff, the Yowie finally retreated into the darkness, its growls fading away. Seizing the moment, the guys quickly dragged a heavy cabinet over in front of the damaged wall, hoping it would provide some extra protection.

Jason and Charlie returned to the living room, tired but determined. "It's not over yet," Jason said, his voice grim. "But at least we bought ourselves some time."

Lydia and Kayla looked at them with a mixture of relief and anxiety. "Hopefully the flare made it think twice." Kayla asked, her voice barely above a whisper.

The group settled back into their vigil, fear still lingering but tempered by their resolve. They knew the Yowie was still out there, but they knew they would fight back, no matter what it took.

CHAPTER 19

The group were sitting quietly on the couch and floor when the silence was shattered by another series of heavy thuds against the side of the cottage. The Yowie was testing the weak points of their defenses, looking for any way to get inside.

"We need to reinforce that side," Jason said, his voice strained with exhaustion. "It's only a matter of time before it breaks through."

"Do we even have anything left to use?" Charlie asked, frustration creeping into his voice. "We're running out of options."

Kayla looked around, her mind racing. "We need to find something, anything that can hold it off."

They quickly worked together, using furniture from

the other rooms to brace the windows and doors securely. Lydia and Kayla joined in, handing them anything that could help reinforce the walls.

Retreating back to the living room, fear and exhaustion weighed heavily on them, but they knew they couldn't give up.

"We need to stay quiet and use the lights we have left," Charlie suggested. "It's sensitive to light. We will use that to our advantage."

"What if that doesn't work?" Jason snapped, his frustration boiling over. "We're just sitting here, waiting for it to break in and kill us!"

"Do you have a better idea?" Charlie shot back, his patience wearing thin. "We need to work together, not tear each other apart."

"Enough!" Lydia interjected, stepping between them. "We're all scared and exhausted but fighting among ourselves won't help. We need to stay focused."

Kayla, trying to calm the group, said, "Let's use the flares. They worked before to keep it at bay. If it comes too close, we throw them. Let the bugger burn."

The group calmed down, each person grabbing a flare.

Another hour passed, when suddenly the Yowie returned with a vengeance, its growls louder and more menacing than ever. It then unleashed a piercing, relentless scream that vibrated through the very walls of the cottage. The intensity of the sound made their ears ring and disoriented the group. As the scream morphed into a siren-like wail, the noise left them feeling nauseous and overwhelmed.

The group covered their ears, trying to block out the horrific noise. "It's trying to drive us out!" Lydia shouted over the noise, as she pressed her hands over her ears.

The Yowie's scream-siren grew louder, lasting for what felt like an hour, until the group felt nauseous and dizzy. Then, with a mighty crash, the creature punched through the bookshelf that was blocking the already shattered window. The bookshelf fell to the floor with a resounding thud, scattering debris everywhere.

Despite the overwhelming feeling of nausea, Kayla forced herself to her feet. She grabbed a flare, ignited it, and threw it through the window at the Yowie, screaming, "Burn you monster!" The creature recoiled, but before it could react further, Charlie followed suit, lighting and throwing his flare with shaking hands.

Both flares hit the Yowie in the chest and face, quickly igniting the oily hair over its body. The creature let out a god-awful scream, a sound that was even more horrifying than before, as the flames consumed it.

The group watched in a mix of horror and relief as the Yowie retreated into the bush, well alight, its screams echoing through the night. As it ran, it set alight a few bushes, the flames flickering eerily until they finally faded into the distance.

"We did it," Jason said, relief evident in his voice. "We actually did it."

The group slumped to the floor, exhaustion overtaking them. They had survived the night, but the damage to the cottage and their own battered nerves was evident.

"We need to assess the damage," Lydia said, her voice shaky but determined. "Make sure we're safe."

They moved through the cottage, checking the barricades and the walls. The Yowie had caused considerable damage, but the structure was still standing. They pushed the bookshelf back up against the shattered window and settled back into the living room, sharing a moment of quiet triumph. They had faced the Yowie and survived, but they knew their ordeal might not be over.

"Do you think it's gone for good?" Kayla asked, her voice filled with hope and uncertainty.

Jason exhaled deeply and replied, "I bloody hope so."

CHAPTER 20

As the first rays of sunlight pierced through the remnants of the night, the group lay resting in the living room. They hadn't slept, too scared to let their guard down. The terror of the previous hours still clung to them, but the dawn brought a sense of hope.

As the light grew, Jason slowly stood, stretching his stiff limbs. "The sun's up," he said, his voice hoarse. "We should check the damage."

The others nodded, rising to their feet. They moved around the house, inspecting the barricades and the shattered window. The signs of the Yowie's assault were everywhere—splintered wood, broken furniture, and scattered debris.

They gathered by the living room window, peering outside to see if there was any sign of the creature. The bush beyond was calm, bathed in the soft light of the morning.

"I don't see anything," Charlie said, relief mixed with caution in his voice.

"Charlie, we should do a walk around the perimeter," Jason suggested. "Make sure it's really gone."

Charlie agreed, and the two men grabbed their weapons before heading outside, leaving Lydia and Kayla in the living room. The women watched them go, their nerves still on edge.

Jason and Charlie moved cautiously around the house, stepping over broken branches and debris. The outside of the cottage was a mess, with claw marks gouging the walls and patches of scorched earth where the flares had hit their target.

"It really did a number on the place," Charlie remarked, kicking at a piece of broken wood.

"And it really did a number on us too," Jason added, her voice filled with a mixture of weariness and resolve.

"There's no sign of it, though," Charlie replied, scanning the tree line. "Maybe we scared it off for good."

They completed their circuit and returned to the living room. "The outside is a mess, but no sign of the Yowie," Jason reported.

Lydia exhaled a sigh of relief. "Let's have some coffee.

We need something to steady our nerves."

She moved to the kitchen, preparing strong coffee for everyone and a hot chocolate for Kayla. The warm drinks helped calm their nerves and allowed them to focus on the moment.

An hour later, they were resting in the living room, trying to regain some semblance of calm. The sun was higher in the sky now, casting bright light through the windows.

The silence was broken by the distant sound of engines. The group tensed, listening intently. As the noise grew closer, they heard the unmistakable sound of cars approaching.

"Oh my god, do you hear that?" Kayla wondered aloud, her eyes wide with excitement.

"Finally," Jason said, standing up. The others followed him outside, their hearts pounding with hope.

They stepped out into the morning light, squinting against the brightness. Two SUV's were approaching, sliding a little as they came down the muddy road towards the cottage.

CHAPTER 21

The crisp morning air filled their lungs as the vehicles came to a halt in front of the cottage. The door of the lead car opened, and Susan Murray, the cottage owner, stepped out. Her eyes widened in shock at the sight of the cottage. Following her in the second SUV was a uniformed policeman, his face set in a serious expression.

Susan approached, her gaze sweeping over the damage—splintered wood, shattered windows, and the remains of their defensive efforts. She looked back at the group, her expression a mix of concern and apology.

"Are you all okay?" she asked, her voice shaking slightly. "I'm so sorry about all of this. When I got home, I saw the damage to my house and called the police before coming here."

Jason stepped forward, nodding. "We're managing, but

it was a rough night. We're glad to see you."

The policeman stepped closer, his stern gaze softening as he assessed the situation. "I'm Officer Daniels. Susan called us when she saw the state of her place. What happened here?"

"Maybe you should come inside and see for yourselves," Jason replied.

As they made their way back into the living room, Susan took in the chaos—the overturned furniture, the hastily constructed barricades, and the exhaustion etched on everyone's faces. "My God," she whispered, "I can't believe this happened."

"We can't either," Kayla replied.

They settled into what seats were still usable, and Lydia began recounting the events of the night. "It had been harassing us over the past couple of nights and last night, or this morning rather, it tried to get in."

The policeman looked puzzled. "What tried to get in?"

"A Yowie, officer. A freaking Yowie," Jason replied, his voice filled with a mix of frustration and disbelief.

Charlie chimed in, his voice still shaky from the ordeal. "We tried to reinforce the windows and doors, but it was so strong. We used flares to drive it away, but it kept coming back."

Kayla added, "It screamed—like nothing I've ever heard. The sound was so intense it made us feel sick. We barely managed to hold it off until morning."

Susan listened, her face paling as the details unfolded. "I had no idea… I'm so sorry you all went through this."

Officer Daniels took notes, his brow furrowed. "This creature—can you describe it in more detail? Any specific features that stood out?"

Jason nodded. "It was massive, covered in thick hair. Bigger than you can imagine. Its eyes glowed in the dark, and it seemed almost intelligent in how it tried to break in. It was relentless."

Susan took a deep breath, her hands shaking. "I need to confess something. I think I know why it was so aggressive. About two months ago, I started seeing signs of it around the property. At first, I was terrified, but then I began leaving food out for it, hoping it would stay away from the house."

Kayla's eyes widened in realisation. "You were feeding it?"

Susan nodded, guilt etched into her features. "I left to go out of town and forgot to put out the food before I left. I was in such a rush and stressed about going to see my sister in the hospital. I think that's why it was so angry. It came looking for the food and got mad because there wasn't any there for it."

Kayla's face turned red with anger. "You caused this! We could have died because you were feeding it and then stopped. Do you realise how dangerous that was?"

Charlie, his frustration boiling over, added, "You put us in danger. We had no idea what we were walking into. This whole nightmare could have been avoided."

Susan's eyes filled with tears. "I am so sorry. I never meant for anyone to get hurt. I thought I was helping, but I see now how wrong I was."

Officer Daniels stepped in. "We need to focus on what we do next. Blame won't help us right now. We need to ensure everyone's safety and figure out how to deal with this creature."

"With all due respect, Officer Daniels, all we care about is getting the hell out of here," Jason said, looking around at his family.

"That would be best," Lydia agreed. "We need to rest somewhere safe. As you would have seen, our car needs a new windscreen, and Margaret, you need a new BBQ."

Officer Daniels nodded. "Grab your stuff. I'll organise for someone to tow your SUV into town and get the windscreen fixed so you can head home tomorrow."

"Sounds good," Jason replied. "We'll get rooms at a local motel until the windscreen is fixed."

Once they had packed their belongings, the group followed Susan and Officer Daniels outside. The fresh morning air was refreshing, a stark contrast to the fear-laden night they had endured. They loaded their bags into the cars, casting one last glance at the ravaged cottage.

Susan looked back at the house, her eyes glistening with unshed tears. "I promise I will make this right. I'll do whatever it takes to ensure this never happens again."

As they were about to get into the cars, Officer Daniels turned to the group. "There's something you should know. We've had reports of Yowies in this area before, but officially, we can't let that be known. It would cause a lot of panic and trouble. Can I count on you all to keep what happened here to yourselves?"

The group exchanged looks, the weight of their ordeal still heavy on their shoulders. Jason spoke for all of them. "We just want to forget this ever happened, Officer. You have our word."

Officer Daniels nodded, relief evident in his eyes. "Thank you. Let's get you to the station to give a statement and then you can head to the motel to rest."

The ride to the station was quiet, each person lost in their thoughts. The ordeal had taken its toll, and the reality of what they had survived was beginning to sink in. When they arrived, Officer Daniels led them inside, arranging for them to give their statements.

They agreed to describe the creature as a wild animal

and admitted they never got a clear look at it. After giving their statements, they felt a mix of relief and exhaustion. Once they were done, Susan offered to drive them to the motel.

Susan was determined to support the group she had unknowingly placed in danger. As they arrived at the motel, they thanked Susan for her help.

"I'll cover the cost of the motel and refund the costs you paid for the cottage. It's the least I can do after what you've been through," Susan said, her voice filled with regret.

"Thank you," Kayla replied.

The group checked into the motel, feeling the weight of their exhaustion. They made their way to their rooms, finally able to rest in a place where they felt safe.

The group, while still shaken, felt a sense of solidarity and determination. They had faced a nightmare and survived, and now it was time to rest.

CHAPTER 22

The next morning, the group woke up in the motel, feeling a mix of exhaustion and relief. They were ready to leave this nightmare behind and return to the safety and comfort of their homes.

Jason, Lydia, Kayla, and Charlie gathered in the motel lobby, bags packed and expressions weary but hopeful. Susan had arranged for breakfast to be delivered, and they ate in relative silence, each lost in their thoughts about the ordeal they had survived.

As they finished their meal, Officer Daniels arrived.

"Morning," Officer Daniels greeted them. "How are you all holding up?"

"Better," Jason replied. "Just looking forward to getting home."

Officer Daniels said, "I'm sorry your stay wasn't better. But I've made sure your SUV is ready to go. The windscreen has been fixed, and it should be good as new," he added, pointing to the car now waiting in the carpark.

"Thank you," Lydia said. "We appreciate everything you've done."

"Remember," Officer Daniels said, "if you need anything, don't hesitate to call. We'll continue to monitor the area and make sure it's safe."

"Thanks, Officer," Jason said. "We'll definitely do that."

With their SUV packed and ready, the group climbed in. Jason started the engine, and they pulled away from the motel, leaving behind the site of their ordeal.

As they drove, they could finally breathe easier. The miles rolled by, and the familiarity of the surroundings brought a sense of comfort. They talked quietly among themselves, reflecting on the events and their relief at being on their way home.

"I can't believe we went through all of that," Kayla said, staring out the window. "It feels like a bad dream."

"A bad dream we survived, thankfully," Lydia replied.

Charlie leaned back in his seat, closing his eyes. "I just want to forget it ever happened."

Jason glanced at him in the rear view mirror. "Me too,

brother."

The rest of the drive was quiet but peaceful. They passed through small towns and open countryside, each mile bringing them closer to the safety and comfort of home. When they finally pulled into their neighbourhood, a collective sigh of relief filled the SUV.

Jason parked in front of Kayla's and Charlie's house. "Here you are guys," he said, turning off the engine. "Home sweet home."

They climbed out of the SUV, stretching and breathing in the familiar air. The nightmare they had endured was finally behind them, and they were ready to move forward.

Before parting ways, they stood together in the driveway, a sense of unity and strength binding them.

"We'll always have each other," Lydia said, her voice filled with emotion. "No matter what happens."

Jason nodded. "We faced something terrible, but we came through it together. And that's what matters."

With hugs and reassurances, they said their goodbyes. Jason and Kayla headed to their home, while Jason and Lydia drove to their home only five minutes away.

As Jason and Kayla walked up to their front door, Kayla turned to him. "Do you think we'll ever see something like that again?"

Jason shook his head. "I hope not. I've never felt so grateful for living in suburbia."

With a final hug, they stepped inside, closing the door on the nightmare they had faced. They were home, safe and together, ready to move forward into a brighter future.

EPILOGUE

The Yowie stumbled through the dense underbrush, its once-mighty strides now weakened by pain. The flames from the flares had seared its flesh, leaving deep burns that still smouldered with a dull, throbbing agony. Its growls echoed through the forest, a mix of rage and suffering, as it made its way back to its hidden cave deep within the Pilliga.

The cave was a sanctuary of shadows and cool, damp air. As the Yowie collapsed onto the rocky floor, its breaths ragged and laboured, a pair of gentle hands reached out to tend to its wounds. A female Yowie, smaller in stature but no less fierce, had been waiting in the cave. She had sensed his distress and prepared a mix of herbs and poultices to ease his suffering. Her presence soothed his pain, and she worked tirelessly to care for him, her touch both tender and skilled.

Days turned into weeks as the male Yowie lay in the darkness, licking his wounds and drawing strength from the solitude. Slowly, his flesh began to heal, the burns transforming into thick, scarred tissue. The female Yowie, always by his side, ensured he had the nourishment and care needed to recover. Her silent companionship was a source of comfort, and together, they forged a bond of mutual support and resilience.

As the pain subsided, a new fire ignited within the creature—a burning desire for revenge. The memory of the humans who had dared to challenge it, to harm it, fueled its rage. Their faces, twisted in fear, were etched into its mind. The Yowie had always avoided human contact, understanding that its survival depended on secrecy and stealth. However, it had grown accustomed to the food that was regularly placed outside for it on that farm.

But these humans had crossed a line, and the Yowie could not let their actions go unanswered.

During his recovery, the Yowie's mind was consumed by thoughts of retribution. He replayed the events of that fateful night over and over again, analysing every detail. He remembered the terror in the humans' eyes, the desperation in their voices, and the searing pain of the flares. The Yowie knew that he had to be smarter, more cunning, if he was to exact his revenge. With the help of the female Yowie, who shared his determination, they began to devise a plan, one that would ensure the humans paid dearly for their transgressions.

The Yowie's senses grew sharper as his body healed. He listened intently to the sounds of the forest, the rustling of leaves, the calls of birds, and the distant howls of other creatures. He used these sounds to gauge the passage of time and to monitor the movements of potential threats. The Yowie knew that patience was key, and he was willing to wait as long as necessary to strike back at the humans.

As the days turned into weeks, the Yowie's resolve only grew stronger. He honed his hunting skills, stalking prey with precision and cunning. He left subtle marks and signs in the forest, warnings to other creatures to stay away. The Yowies' presence was felt throughout the Pilliga, a silent reminder of their dominance.

One evening, as the sun dipped below the horizon, the Yowie caught the scent of something familiar. It was faint, but unmistakable—the scent of humans. His heart quickened with anticipation as he followed the trail, his senses heightened and alert. The scent led him to a campsite, where the remnants of a fire still smouldered.

The Yowie observed the campsite from a distance, his eyes narrowing as he took in the scene. There were no humans in sight, but their presence was unmistakable. The Yowie could see the signs of their activities—footprints in the dirt, discarded food wrappers, and the faint hum of electronic devices. He knew that the humans would return, and he was ready to confront them. They weren't the humans that had scarred him, but they would do, for now.

The Yowie waited in the shadows, his breath steady and controlled. He watched as the humans returned to the campsite, their voices carrying through the night air. They seemed relaxed, unaware of the danger that lurked nearby.

The Yowie bided his time, waiting for the perfect moment to strike. He observed the humans closely, learning their routines and patterns. He noted their weaknesses and vulnerabilities, and he devised a plan to exploit them. The female Yowie, always by his side, watched with a steely determination, ready to support him when the time came.

As the humans settled around the campfire, the Yowie made his move. He approached the campsite with stealth and precision, his massive form moving silently through the underbrush. He positioned himself behind a large tree, his eyes fixed on the humans. The Yowie could feel his heart pounding in his chest, the anticipation almost unbearable.

With a sudden burst of speed, the Yowie lunged forward, his powerful limbs propelling him toward the humans. The element of surprise was on his side, and the humans had no time to react. The Yowie's roar echoed through the night, a terrifying sound that sent shivers down the spines of his prey.

AUTHOR BIO

Luka T. Jacobs is an author with a passion for cryptids, particularly Sasquatch and Dogman. Originally hailing from Sydney, Australia, Luka now calls the picturesque Illawarra region of New South Wales home, where she resides with her partner and their cheeky little dog, Finnigan.

With a deep love for animals and a keen sense of adventure, Luka's fascination with the mysteries of the natural world fuels her storytelling. Drawing from her background in Graphic Design and Art, she brings a unique visual flair to her writing.

As an avid traveler and explorer of the unknown, Luka continues to seek inspiration from the wild and untamed corners of the world, eager to share her imaginative worlds with readers everywhere.

Facebook: https://www.facebook.com/lukatjacobs

Amazon: https://amazon.com/author/lukatjacobs

Website: http://www.LukaTJacobs.com

NIGHT AT THE ROADHOUSE

IDAHO

My name is Huck and I've been a trucker for over twenty years. Born and raised in Idaho, I've driven these roads more times than I can count. I've seen my fair share of weird things out there, but nothing quite like what happened one chilly November night at a roadhouse just off Highway 95.

I was hauling a load of potatoes down to Boise and decided to pull over for the night. The roadhouse was a popular spot for truckers—a small diner with a big parking lot, always a few rigs parked overnight. I found a spot near the back, turned off the engine, and settled in for some much-needed shut-eye.

The night was clear, and the air had a bite to it, a reminder that winter was here. The parking lot was quieter than usual, with only a few other trucks scattered around. I closed my eyes and tried to drift off, but for some reason, sleep wouldn't come. After tossing and turning for what felt like hours, I finally gave up and decided to get out and have a smoke.

I stepped out of the cab and lit up a cigarette, the ember glowing bright in the dark. The night was eerily quiet, not a sound except for the occasional rustle of leaves in the wind. It was spooky, to be honest, like the calm before a storm. I looked around, seeing the dark shapes of the other trucks silhouetted against the dim glow of the roadhouse's neon sign.

Something didn't feel right, but I couldn't put my finger on it. I don't get spooked easily, so I took a deep drag and tried to shake off the unease, chalking it up to being overtired. After a few minutes, I finished my cigarette, flicked the butt away, and climbed back into the truck. I laid back down, hoping sleep would come easier this time.

It couldn't have been more than twenty minutes later when I was jolted awake by a strange noise. It was a scraping sound, like something dragging across metal, followed by a blowing noise, almost like a deer makes. My heart started pounding in my chest, and I strained to listen. The noise stopped for a moment, then started up again, louder this time.

I sat up in my bunk, peering out the window. The parking lot was dark, and I couldn't see much beyond the dim glow of the diner. The noise continued, scraping and blowing, unnerving me. I'd never heard anything like it before.

Out of my peripheral vision I saw movement between the trucks. At first, I thought it was a wolf, but something was seriously off. It was walking on two legs, hunched over, and had hands similar to a raccoons. It's lower body was skinny but the top half looked like it was pure muscle.

I could only see it from the back, but it was enough to make my blood pressure sky rocket. It was slightly hunched as it sniffed the air, then it headed towards another truck parked a few spaces away.

Is that a freakin' werewolf, I thought.

My brain whirled, attempting to process the sight before me. It looked like a wolf, but wolves don't walk on two legs. I watched in horror as it reached the other truck, disappearing into the shadows. The blowing noise came again, louder and more insistent.

I wanted to get out of there, to start the engine and drive away as fast as I could, but I didn't want it to notice me. I couldn't move, couldn't think. All I could do was sit there, heart pounding, eyes fixed on the spot where the creature had disappeared.

I am 55 years old and nothing has ever terrified me like that creature did.

After a while, the noise stopped. The night was silent again, and I tried to calm my breathing. I laid back down, pulling the blanket up to my chin, ears straining for any sound. I don't know how long I lay there, tense and trembling, but eventually, exhaustion took over, and I drifted off to sleep.

I woke up to the harsh light of morning, the events of the night before feeling like a bad dream. But the unease was still there, a lingering sense of dread that wouldn't go away. I climbed out of the truck, looking around the parking lot. Everything seemed normal, but I couldn't shake the feeling that something was watching me.

I quickly did my pre-trip inspection, eager to get back on the road and put as much distance between me and that roadhouse as possible. As I pulled out of the lot, I vowed never to stop there again. Whatever that thing was, I didn't want to see it again.

In the days and weeks that followed, I couldn't stop thinking about that night. I tried to rationalize it, to convince myself that it was just my imagination, that I was overtired and seeing things. But deep down, I knew what I had seen was real. The memory of that creature, walking on two legs, its movements, haunted me.

I dared to mention my sighting to a few other truckers, but most of them just laughed it off, thinking I was joking around. One old-timer though, stopped me as I was leaving and simply said "what you saw was real".

I was a bit taken aback, but glad I wasn't the only one that had seen this evil-looking creature.

THE FACE UNDER THE PORCH

BRITISH COLUMBIA CA

I've got to tell you a story that's been haunting me for years. My name's Jason, and I'm 26 now, living in Vancouver. I moved here for college, wanting to put some distance between myself and the place where this story takes place. My parents have a rural property outside of Kamloops, BC, and I've hated it ever since we moved there when I was 15. I never could quite explain why—it just never felt right to me. My parents, though, they absolutely love the place.

Recently, I decided it was time for my girlfriend, Emily, to meet my folks. She'd been curious about my reluctance to visit my childhood home and why I seemed uneasy whenever it came up in conversation. I thought maybe facing it head-on would help, so we flew into Kamloops, hired a car, and started the drive out to the property. It was around 7 PM in early May, with the sun just dipping below the horizon.

As we pulled down the long gravel driveway, I felt that familiar knot of unease tighten in my stomach. The driveway was flanked by tall trees on either side, and the house sat at the end like an island of refuge—or, in my case, a place of dread. My parents had installed a motion-operated light on the front porch, but it didn't do much to cut through the encroaching darkness. I even commented to Emily about how useless that light was, trying to mask my nerves with a bit of humor.

We parked and got out of the car. I grabbed Emily's hand, partly for comfort and partly to reassure her. As we walked towards the porch, I stopped suddenly. There was something under the porch, just at the edge of the dim light. I pulled Emily back towards the car quickly, my heart pounding.

"What's wrong?" she asked, her voice tinged with confusion and concern.

"Just get in the car," I said, trying to keep my voice steady. We climbed back in, and I backed up the driveway, not taking my eyes off the porch.

Once we were a safe distance away, Emily demanded to know what had happened. I took a deep breath and tried to calm down before explaining. "When I got closer to the porch, I saw a face under there. At first, I thought it was just a dog or something, but then it grinned at me—like an evil Joker's grin, all teeth and malice. It was like a wolf's face, but not quite. It had this sinister look in its eyes. It's face was pure evil."

Emily looked at me, her eyes wide. "Are you sure it wasn't just a neighbor's dog or something?"

I shook my head. "No way. It was too large and I have never seen a dog look like that thing before. It is like it wanted me to see it and it wanted me to be terrified. I don't know how I know that but I do."

I called my parents from the road and told them what I saw. They were angry and brushed it off, insisting it was probably just a neighbor's dog. I wasn't convinced and refused to go back. We agreed to meet in town at a restaurant instead. Over dinner, I tried to convince them to move, but they were adamant about staying.

The rest of the trip was uneventful, but that encounter refuses to leave my mind. I will never go back to that property.

Emily believed me, and we talked about it here and there, trying to make sense of what I'd seen. To this day, my parents still live there, but I've never set foot on that land again. There's something out there, something that doesn't want me around, and I'm more than happy to oblige.